Cappuccina Goes to Town

To Brendan, Mary Kate, Sophie and Speargrass,
who have taught us to love the grass on our
own side of the fence — M.A.S. & K.S.M.

For Willie, who watches me paint — E.F.

Text © 2002 Mary Ann Smith and Katie Smith Milway
Illustrations © 2002 Eugenie Fernandes

Kids Can Press acknowledges the financial support of the Ontario Arts
Council, the Canada Council for the Arts and the Government of Canada,
through the BPIDP, for our publishing activity.

Published in Canada by
Kids Can Press Ltd.
29 Birch Avenue
Toronto, ON M4V 1E2

Published in the U.S. by
Kids Can Press Ltd.
2250 Military Road
Tonawanda, NY 14150

www.kidscanpress.com

The artwork in this book was rendered in gouache.
The text is set in Celeste.

Edited by Debbie Rogosin
Designed by Karen Powers
Printed and bound in Hong Kong by Book Art Inc., Toronto

This book is smyth sewn casebound.

CM 02 0 9 8 7 6 5 4 3 2 1

National Library of Canada Cataloguing in Publication Data

Smith, Mary Ann
    Cappuccina goes to town

ISBN 1-55074-807-6

I. Milway, Katie Smith, 1960 –.   II. Fernandes, Eugenie, 1943 –.   III. Title.

PS8576.I57438C36 2002   C813'.6   C2001-900999-2
PZ7.M645Ca 2002

Kids Can Press is a Nelvana company

Cappuccina Goes to Town

WRITTEN BY

Mary Ann Smith
& Katie Smith Milway

ILLUSTRATED BY

Eugenie Fernandes

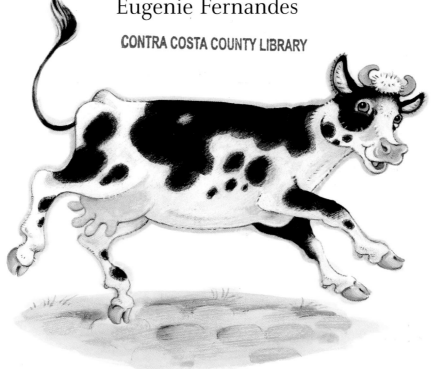

Kids Can Press

Once there was a cow named Cappuccina. She was a white cow with black spots, and she lived in Farmer Fiori's pasture. Cappuccina enjoyed life in the country. But she liked to watch people driving by on their way to town. Sometimes she thought it would be fun to go to town herself. And sometimes she even thought it would be more fun to be a person than a cow.

Yet try as she might, Cappuccina could never find a way beyond the farmyard fence: not under it, not over it, and not around it.

One day after a storm, Cappuccina found a hole in the fence. "This is my chance," she thought. "I will trot through that hole and be off to town."

And so she did.

By the time Cappuccina arrived, her hooves hurt from the stones in the road. "The first thing I must do," she thought, "is buy some shoes."

Cappuccina trotted briskly up to a shoe stall.

"What color shoes would you like?" asked the shoemaker.

And Cappuccina said,

"Blooooooo."

It was her favorite color.

The shoemaker brought out all the blue shoes from his stall. There were blue shoes with buckles and blue shoes with laces and blue shoes with bows. "I'm sure these will do!" he said cheerfully each time Cappuccina tried on a pair. But none of the shoes fit because cows have ... hooves!

"Oh well," thought Cappuccina. "Perhaps I should
get a hat. It's such a hot day." Bowing good-bye, she tripped
next door to the hat stand.

"What kind of hat may I show you?" asked the hatter.
And Cappuccina replied,

"Blooooooo."

In a jiffy, the lady brought out all the blue hats in her stand.

There were blue hats with feathers and blue hats with fruit and blue hats with flowers.

"Maybe if we tilt this one just so," the woman said hopefully as she placed hat after hat on Cappuccina. But try as they might, no hat fit because cows have ... horns.

"That's all right," thought Cappuccina.
"I will get a pretty dress to wear." Tossing her
head in a friendly way, she stepped over to the
dressmaker's.

"What sort of dress are you looking for?" asked the dressmaker. This was the first time she had served a customer like Cappuccina. And Cappuccina said,

"Blooooooo."

The dressmaker picked out all the blue dresses on her rack. There were blue dresses with polka dots and blue dresses with stripes and blue dresses with lacy trim. "Just a little more flounce and we'll have it," she said each time Cappuccina tried on a dress. But in the end, not one dress fit Cappuccina because cows have ... tails.

"Oh my," said Cappuccina to herself. "I can't wear shoes, or hats, or dresses." She was beginning to get discouraged. And she was a little tired.

Then, across the square, she spied a wonderful place to rest. With a tip of her horns, she walked across to the beauty parlor and plopped herself down in a big, comfortable chair.

The hairdresser rushed to her side. "My, my! What color hair would you like?" he asked.

Cappuccina thought for a moment. And then she said ...

"Blooooooo."

After all, it *was* her favorite color.

The hairdresser brought out all the blue wigs in his shop. There were blue wigs with curly tops and blue wigs with long tresses and blue wigs with perky pigtails. But fluff and puff as he might, not one seemed right for Cappuccina.

Finally, the hairdresser had an idea.

He found a blue ribbon and tied
a big bow right on Cappuccina's ... tail!
"There!" said the hairdresser,
holding up a mirror.

"Oooooooooo."

lowed Cappuccina, admiring her tail.
She had wanted to be a person, but she
really was just perfect as herself.

With that happy thought, Cappuccina waved her tail and
pranced out of the shop and around the square. What a day she
had had. And how hungry she was.

She walked past a pizzeria. She walked past a café. And she
walked past a fruit stand. But Cappuccina didn't stop. She knew
what she wanted for supper. And she knew just where to find it.

She walked past the hairdresser's, the dressmaker's, the hatter's and the shoemaker's. She trotted out of town and all the way back to Farmer Fiori's pasture.

Cappuccina was so delighted to be home
that she kicked up her heels and did something
she had never done before. She jumped right
over the fence!

As she pranced through the pasture to her trough, Farmer Fiori came out with some crunchy hay and some sweet alfalfa — exactly what Cappuccina wanted for supper.

"Ah, Cappuccina," said Farmer Fiori, "I've been so busy today that I've hardly seen you!" He scratched her ear where he knew she liked it.

"Your life is so peaceful," he said. "You spend your days
in the field, listening to the birds and smelling the flowers.
Do you know what? Sometimes I wish I were a cow."
And Cappuccina said,

"Moooooooo."